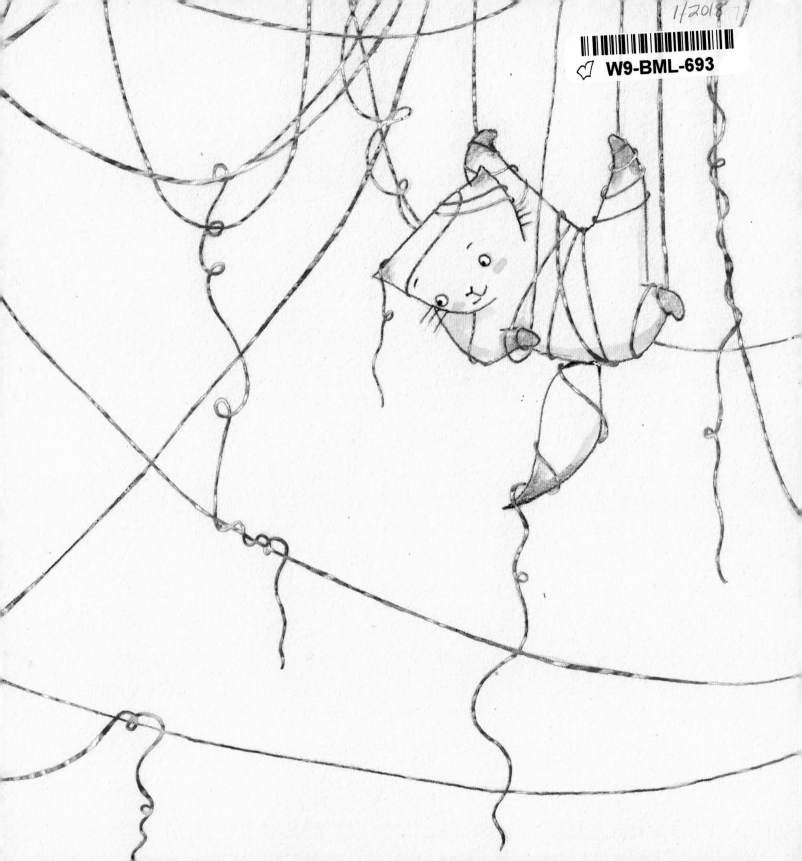

W9-BML-693

Mr. Fluffernutter

Jennifer Gray Olson

Alfred A. Knopf   New York

Mr. Fluffernutter and I
are best friends.

We love spending time together

doing all of our favorite things.

Today we are having a tea party!

Mr. Fluffernutter
LOVES tea parties!

Milk, sugar,
Mr. Fluffernutter?

After tea,
we play…
DRESS-UP!

Looking good,
Mr. Fluffernutter!

He enjoys getting fancy.

We have tons of fun
all morning.

Hey, where are you going,
Mr. Fluffernutter?

It seems like
Mr. Fluffernutter
would rather stare
at the fish today.

Okay, Mr. Fluffernutter.

You want WHAT for lunch,
Mr. Fluffernutter?!

And NOW you just want to play with your yarn?

Maybe Mr. Fluffernutter and I
AREN'T best friends after all.
Maybe we'll have more fun...

alone.

See, that's better.

Much better.

Yup.

Awwwww, Mr.

Fluffernutter!!!

Mr. Fluffernutter and I
BOTH really like bath time.

We just do it
a little differently.

Good night,
Mr. Fluffernutter.

For those who love us,
even at our most unlovable

THIS IS A BORZOI BOOK PUBLISHED BY ALFRED A. KNOPF

Copyright © 2017 by Jennifer Gray Olson

All rights reserved. Published in the United States by Alfred A. Knopf, an imprint of Random House Children's Books,
a division of Penguin Random House LLC, New York.

Knopf, Borzoi Books, and the colophon are registered trademarks of Penguin Random House LLC.

Visit us on the Web! randomhousekids.com

Educators and librarians, for a variety of teaching tools, visit us at RHTeachersLibrarians.com

Library of Congress Cataloging-in-Publication Data is available upon request.

ISBN 978-0-385-75496-5 (trade) — ISBN 978-0-385-75497-2 (lib. bdg.) — ISBN 978-0-385-75498-9 (ebook)

The illustrations in this book were created using pencil, watercolor, and digital collage.

MANUFACTURED IN CHINA

October 2017   10 9 8 7 6 5 4 3 2 1   First Edition

Random House Children's Books supports the First Amendment and celebrates the right to read.